The Case of the
Loose-Toothed Shark

BY **NANCY KRULIK**

ILLUSTRATED BY **GARY LaCOSTE**

SCHOLASTIC INC.

New York   Toronto   London   Auckland
Sydney   Mexico City   New Delhi   Hong Kong

For Amanda, who was always excited
when the tooth fairy came!

No part of this publication may be reproduced, stored in a retrieval system, or
transmitted in any form or by any means, electronic, mechanical, photocopying,
recording, or otherwise, without written permission of the publisher. For information
regarding permission, write to Scholastic Inc., Attention: Permissions Department,
557 Broadway, New York, NY 10012.

ISBN 978-0-545-26657-4

Text copyright © 2012 by Nancy Krulik.
Illustrations copyright © 2012 by Scholastic Inc.
All rights reserved. Published by Scholastic Inc.
SCHOLASTIC and associated logos are trademarks
and/or registered trademarks of Scholastic Inc.

12 11 10 9 8 7 6 5 4 3 2   12 13 14 15 16 17/0

Printed in the U.S.A.   40
First printing, February 2012
Book design by Yaffa Jaskoll

Chapter 1

"MOMMY!" my sister Mia whined as we walked into the aquarium on Saturday. "Jack's not wearing my birthday party T-shirt!"

I thought about throwing my jacket back on so my mother couldn't see that I was wearing my Houston Astros jersey, but it was too late.

My mother sighed. "Jack, we talked about this," she warned.

"I know," I said. "But I always wear my Astros shirt to birthday parties. It's my have-fun-at-a-party shirt."

"This is Mia's day, Jack," my mom said. "Can't you just wear the T-shirt?"

Mom wasn't really asking. She was *telling*. So I took off my Astros shirt and pulled Mia's birthday shirt out

1

of my backpack and slipped it on over my undershirt. I shoved the Astros jersey into my pack.

I was glad none of my friends was there to see me wearing a pink T-shirt that read *I Did Something Fishy at Mia's Birthday Party*. Luckily, the aquarium didn't open to the public until noon. So for now the only people I'd be seeing were Mia's friends and the aquarium workers.

Just then, I heard someone complaining.

"Get away from my gravel!" he shouted.

I turned to find out who it was, but the only thing I saw was an enormous fish tank with a crab sitting at the bottom.

Two clown fish swam into view.

"Hoho, what do you call someone who lives in the sea, is grouchy, and hates neighbors?" one clown fish asked the other.

"I don't know, Bobo," Hoho said.

"A hermit crab," Bobo answered.

"Grrr . . ." the crab grumbled. He shoved his head back into his shell. "I hate clown fish!"

I laughed. Those fish were pretty funny.

"MOM!" Mia shouted out. "Jack's making fun of me."

"I didn't say anything," I told her.

"You laughed," Mia said.

"I wasn't laughing at you," I told her. "I was laughing at —" I stopped myself. What was I supposed to say? I was laughing at two clown fish joking around with a crab?

But it was the truth. I'd understood every word the fish had said. That's because I can talk to animals. No, really. I can.

It all started one day when I was taking my dog, Scout, out for a walk in the front yard, and two squirrels were up in a tree having target practice with some acorns. Unfortunately, my head was the target, and they got me good.

Ordinarily, the only thing an acorn bash to the head would have left me with would have been a lump. But the oak tree in my front yard is a magic tree. *Seriously.* If a human is hit with an acorn from that tree, he gets special powers — like being able to talk to animals.

A magic tree? I didn't believe it at first, either. But the squirrels told me about it. And once I realized I could understand two squirrels, I figured there was something to their story about the magic tree. Ever since that day, I've been able to talk to all kinds of animals. Even fish.

"Jack, come here," my mother said. She was standing next to a tall, skinny woman with long, dark hair. The woman was wearing a blue shirt that read *Friend of the Fishes: Seaside Aquarium.*

"This is Alyssa, Mia's party helper," my mother explained. "She has a surprise for you."

"Why does Jack get a surprise?" Mia demanded. "It's *my* birthday."

"We have surprises for you, too," Alyssa assured Mia. "But you have to be at least eight for this one."

"I'm nine," I announced.

"Then you're old enough to swim with our sharks!" Alyssa told me.

Yikes. That sounded scary. *And* dangerous. "You want me to get into a tank with a bunch of giant, man-eating sharks?" I asked.

I gave my mom a funny look. This was the same woman who didn't like to let me sled down steep hills or jump off the high diving board at the neighborhood pool. Now she was going to let me swim with killer sharks? It didn't make any sense.

Alyssa laughed. "Our sharks aren't giant or man-eating. They're sandbar sharks. They only grow to be about three to four feet long."

Those were my kind of sharks. "When can I dive in?" I asked.

"In a little while," Alyssa said. "You can swim with the sharks while Mia and her friends watch a puppet show."

My mom took my swim trunks out of her pocketbook. "I snuck these from your drawer," she explained. "I wanted the shark swim to be a surprise."

Mia scowled. "I don't want Jack to swim if I can't," she said. "It's *my* birthday."

"Mia, you're six now," Mom scolded. "You need to act more mature. Come on. Let's see how your cake turned out."

Double wow. I sure wished my best friend, Leo, was here to see this. Not only was I going to swim with sharks, but my mom had yelled at Mia the Pain on her birthday! Maybe this day wasn't going to be as awful as I had thought.

"MOM!" I heard Mia whining again from down the hall.

Grrr. Or maybe it *would* still be awful. After all, I was going to be trapped in a sea of kindergartners for the entire morning.

Chapter 2

"Hi, Jack!"

Suddenly, I heard a voice behind me. It wasn't a fish voice or a crab voice. It was the voice of the smartest girl I knew, Elizabeth Morrison.

"Hi," I said. "What are you doing here?"

Elizabeth shot me a goofy smile. I hate that. It looks like she likes me or something. I definitely do not like her — at least not like that. I only like Elizabeth like a partner. Which is what she is. My *detective* partner.

Yup, Elizabeth and I solve mysteries. We're pretty good, too. We've already solved three cases. We found Leo's science fair plans after they'd been stolen. We rescued my sister's tortoise, Tut, after he had been kidnapped. We also caught the prankster who turned the school guinea pig green. We're practically professionals.

But there weren't any mysteries going on right now. Unless of course you counted the mystery of why the smartest girl in the third grade was at my little sister's birthday party.

"My little brother, Alfred, was invited to Mia's party," Elizabeth explained. "Your mom invited me as your guest."

"Oh." If my mom had told me I could bring a guest, I would have invited Leo. He's really fun to have around. But Elizabeth was better than no one. She was actually pretty nice, once you got to know her.

"Elizabeth, I'm scared," Alfred whined.

I looked at him. "What's scary about fish?"

Alfred shook his head so hard his red hair fell in his eyes. "It's not the fish," he said. "It's the tsunami. That's a giant wave that destroys everything in its path."

"That won't happen here," Elizabeth assured him. "You need an underwater volcanic eruption to make a tsunami. There aren't any volcanoes in those tanks."

The Brainiacs sure had some weird conversations. But Elizabeth had made Alfred feel better. He ran off to play with the other kindergartners.

"He's such a worrier," Elizabeth said. "I guess it's because he's so smart."

I shrugged. It was possible. He was part of the Brainiac family, after all.

"You want to explore?" Elizabeth asked me. "I'd like to learn all about the sharks before we swim with them. I'm not *you*. I can't just ask them questions."

Elizabeth is the only person who knows I can talk to animals. I haven't even told Leo, because I'm afraid he'll think I'm really weird. I actually never *told* Elizabeth about it, either — she's just such a Brainiac that she figured it out on her own.

"Sure," I agreed. "My parents said I can explore the aquarium as long as I come back to the party in time for the cake."

"Sounds good to me," Elizabeth said.

As Elizabeth and I walked down the hall, we spotted a giant squid hanging from the ceiling. It was huge — the size of my school bus!

"Amazing!" Elizabeth gasped.

"I wonder how many fishermen it took to drag that thing in," I said.

"Probably a lot," Elizabeth said. She walked a little farther down the hall, and then stopped in front of what looked like a giant triangular-shaped brown rock.

"What's that?" I asked.

A kid with a Mohawk haircut walked over before Elizabeth could answer. "It's a megalodon shark tooth fossil," he said.

"A shark tooth?" I asked nervously. The thing was the size of a cell phone!

"Relax," Elizabeth said. She read the sign on the wall. "This is a fossil from a twenty-million-year-old shark. Sharks today don't have teeth this big."

"Yeah," the kid with the Mohawk agreed. "Most

shark teeth are much smaller. People wear them as charms on necklaces. You couldn't walk around with that thing around your neck."

"No," I agreed. "But I'd sure like to have it in my bedroom. How cool would that be?"

"*Very* cool," the kid with the Mohawk said. "And expensive. Shark tooth fossils cost a lot of money."

"How do you know so much about shark teeth?" Elizabeth asked him.

"My dad works here," the kid said. "I help out sometimes. I'm Teddy."

"I'm Jack. And this is Elizabeth," I said. "We're here for my sister's birthday."

"You actually have a job here?" Elizabeth asked. She sounded impressed.

"Sort of," Teddy said. "You can't have a real job when you're in sixth grade. But my dad pays me to do chores, which is great, because I'm saving up for a bike. Are you guys going to swim with the sharks later?"

We nodded.

"I'll swim with you," he said. "I can swim in the tanks any time I want."

"Right now, I need to check in at the party," Elizabeth told Teddy and me. "Alfred seemed nervous before."

"Alyssa took the kids up to the fifth floor to see the baby eels," Teddy said. "It's the first stop at every party."

"Thanks," Elizabeth said. "We'll see you later."

"Yup," Teddy agreed. "Meet you in the shark tank!"

A few minutes later, Elizabeth and I found Mia and her friends watching electric eels swim in a tank.

"I wanna touch one!" Mia started to stick her hand in the tank. Alyssa stopped her just in time.

"Those land creatures are *so* annoying," I heard one electric eel say.

"Their behavior is shocking!" his friend agreed.

Just then, Elizabeth grabbed my arm. "Jack! I've got a problem," she exclaimed. "Alfred is missing!"

Chapter 3

I looked around at the crowd of little kids. There wasn't one redheaded Brainiac in the bunch.

Oh no! Elizabeth and I had found missing homework and a kidnapped tortoise. But we had never solved a mystery this big. And I wasn't sure I could.

"What am I going to do?" Elizabeth asked me nervously.

What was she asking *me* for? She was the Brainiac. She should have known what to do.

"Well, you could take out your detective notebook and start writing down clues," I suggested.

"Are you kidding?" Elizabeth demanded. "We don't have time for that!"

"Whatcha doin'?" a small voice asked us.

Elizabeth whipped around. "Alfred!" she shouted. "Where have you been?"

"It takes a long time to walk all the way up to the fifth floor," Alfred explained.

"Why didn't you just take the elevator with everyone else?" I asked him.

Elizabeth sighed. "Alfred doesn't take elevators," she said. "They scare him."

"The cable could break, and then because of gravity, the elevator could fall to the ground." Alfred looked at me. "You know about gravity, right, Jack?"

"Sure," I told him. "We learned that in science class."

"Alfred, go hang out with the other kids." Elizabeth sounded tired.

"Well, that's a mystery solved," I said as he ran off. "And we didn't even have to do anything."

Just then Alyssa clapped her hands three times. The kindergarten kids clapped back and quieted down. "Okay, let's go back to the first floor. I want to show you our turtle pond."

Lucky for Alfred, this time the party walked down the stairs instead of taking the elevator. Elizabeth and I tagged along behind my mom and dad.

"I have a tortoise," Mia told Alyssa as we walked downstairs. "His name is Tut. A tortoise looks like a turtle but they aren't the same. Turtles have to live in or near the water. But tortoises don't."

I frowned. I was the one who had told her that. Now here she was bragging like she had learned it all by herself. But I didn't say anything. It was Mia's birthday. I could let her feel smart for one day.

When we reached the first floor, Alyssa led us into the hall with the giant squid. We had to go through the hall to get to the turtles.

"Wow!" The kids all gasped as they looked up. The squid had looked huge to me. But to little kids like them, it must have seemed enormous.

"That's a giant squid," Alyssa told them. "It lives deep in the ocean."

"When it's alive," Alfred pointed out. "But that one's dead."

"Gross," Mia groaned. "I don't like dead things."

"I've seen lots of dead things," Alfred said. "Like at the natural history museum."

"It's not a dead squid," Alyssa assured the kids. "It's a life-size model."

"Ooh. Don't say 'dead,'" Mia whined.

"I think we should move on," my dad recommended.

"Let's go look at the huge shark tooth," Alyssa said, hurrying the kids away from the squid before Alfred could freak anyone else out. "This shark tooth is actually a fossil. That means it is from a long time ago. This tooth is twenty million years old."

"That's older than you, Daddy," Mia said. My dad laughed.

"The tooth —" Alyssa began. Then she stopped and stared at the shelf. "The tooth is gone!" she exclaimed. "It's been stolen!"

Frank the guard ran over. "Oh no," he said. "It must have happened while I was in the other room."

"Did you see anyone in here before it disappeared?" Alyssa asked.

Frank thought for a minute. "Yeah, a couple of kids. One of them was really interested in it." He looked around and then pointed. "There he is."

I turned to look in the direction where Frank was pointing. But there was no one there. And when I turned back, I realized everyone was staring right at *me*.

Chapter 4

"Me?" I asked nervously. "I didn't steal anything. Why would I steal a shark tooth fossil?"

"I heard you tell Teddy and that girl over there how you'd want to have a giant shark tooth fossil in your room," Frank the guard said.

Everyone stared at me.

"Did you say that, Jack?" my mother asked me.

"Yeah, but I didn't mean I'd steal it," I told her. "I just said it was cool. And it was. *Really* cool."

"I want to see the cool shark tooth!" Mia whined. "It's my birthday, and now I don't get to see the shark tooth. It's all Jack's fault."

That's why I call her Mia the Pain.

"It's not my fault. I didn't steal it," I insisted. "I didn't steal anything." I opened up my backpack and showed them the inside. There was nothing in there but a few baseball cards, my Astros jersey, and my bathing suit. "See?" I said.

"You're ruining my birthday party!" Mia shouted at me.

"I'm not ruining anything," I insisted.

"Are too," Mia said. She crossed her arms across her chest and stuck her tongue out at me.

"Shut up!" I shouted at her.

"MOM!" Mia shouted. "Jack said 'shut up.' We're never supposed to say 'shut up'. You said so."

My mother rolled her eyes. "Maybe we should move on to the turtle pond?" she suggested to Alyssa.

Alyssa nodded. "Come on, kids," she said to the kindergartners.

As the kids left, I turned to my mom and dad. "I didn't take it. I swear," I told them.

My dad looked at me. "If you say you didn't take it, you didn't take it," he said. But he didn't sound 100 percent sure.

"We have to go help with the little kids," my mother told Elizabeth and me. "We can talk about this later."

As my parents walked off, I sat down on a bench near the giant freshwater fish tank on the wall. Elizabeth sat down next to me and put her hand on my shoulder.

"I know you didn't steal anything," she said.

Just then I heard kissing noises.

"Kiss. Kiss. Smooch! I love you," someone said.

"No, I love *you*," someone else added.

Oh great. That was all I needed.

"We are *not* kissy faces!" I shouted out. I pushed Elizabeth's hand off my shoulder.

Frank the guard stared at me. "Who are you talking to?" he asked.

I looked around. There was no one there except me, Elizabeth, and the fish.

"I swear I heard someone say 'I love you,'" I said.

Frank wagged his finger at me. "You're a troublemaker," he told me.

Elizabeth laughed and pointed to two white fish near the front of the tank. They looked like they were kissing. "Those are guorami fish," she said. "They're also called *kissing fish*."

Frank scratched his head. "Crazy kid," he muttered as he walked into the next room.

Talk about embarrassing. The fish had been speaking to each other. I was the only person who had heard them, which was why Frank thought I was nuts. Not that I blamed him. I would have thought I was nuts, too, if I didn't know what had happened.

Frank gave me a nasty look. "I'm going to the office to report the missing shark tooth," he told me. "But you'd better not go far, kid. I'm keeping my eye on you. You might not have that tooth in your backpack. But I bet you stashed it somewhere."

"You don't have any proof of that," Elizabeth said.

"No, but I have a hunch," Frank answered her. "I've been at this a long time, and my hunches are usually right."

Not this time, I thought. But I didn't say that out loud. Frank the guard was too scary.

"I know every inch of this place," Frank continued. "I'm going to find out where you hid that tooth. Mark my words."

Everyone in the aquarium thought I was some sort of crook. It was a really rotten feeling. This party was turning out to be even worse than I'd expected.

"I knew I should have worn my Astros shirt," I grumbled under my breath.

"What?" Elizabeth asked me.

"Never mind," I told her. "We don't have time to talk. We have a new mystery on our hands. We have to find out who stole that tooth — and fast!"

My partner nodded. "I was just thinking the same thing," she said.

Chapter 5

"Okay, let me get out my detective notebook," Elizabeth said. She reached into her backpack and handed me a candy cane–striped felt hat. "Hold this," she said.

"What's this for?" I asked.

Elizabeth shrugged. "In case it gets cold," she said. "I always like to be prepared." She handed me two plastic bags.

"Let me guess," I said. "In case you suddenly get asked to be a dog walker and you have to scoop poop."

"Plastic bags are actually good for a lot of things," Elizabeth said. "I could use one if I wanted to bring home an extra piece of birthday cake."

I guess that made a lot more sense, seeing as how we were at a birthday party. Still, I wasn't going to start carrying plastic bags in my backpack. I was the kind of kid who would just eat that extra slice of cake right there at the party.

"Okay, here we go," Elizabeth said. She opened the notebook to a fresh page.

THE CASE OF THE MISSING SHARK TOOTH

Elizabeth and I were now officially on the case!

But before we could get started, Teddy walked over to us. "What are you guys up to?" he asked.

"We're solving a mystery," I told him. "We're detectives."

Teddy gave us a funny look. "You're kidding, right?"

"We never joke about mysteries," Elizabeth told him. "They're serious business."

"And this one is *really* serious," I said. "That security guard thinks I stole the megalodon shark tooth. And my parents might sort of believe him."

"Well, did you?" Teddy asked me.

"No way!" I declared. I was angry he'd even asked me that.

"I wouldn't bother wasting a whole day trying to figure out who did," Teddy told us. "It could have been anyone."

"But the aquarium will want it back," Elizabeth said. "And we can help."

"They can buy another one," Teddy told her. "They have plenty of money. People donate to the aquarium all the time."

"But I don't want people going around thinking that I stole the shark tooth," I said. "So we have to find out who did."

Teddy shrugged. "Suit yourself. I'm going out to watch the sea lion show. You can come if you want."

I would have loved to see the sea lion show. But this mystery was too important.

"Maybe we can catch a show later," I told him.

"Okay," Teddy said. "But I hope you'll still be able to swim with the sharks."

"We will," Elizabeth assured him. "We'll solve this one fast. We're very good at detective work."

I was glad Elizabeth was so confident. I sure wasn't. We had a case, but we didn't have any clues. Or any suspects.

"Okay, let's get started," Elizabeth said as Teddy walked away. "What do we know so far?"

"Not much," I said. "Except the fossilized tooth disappeared. And I didn't take it."

Elizabeth wrote that down. "That's not much," she admitted. "Luckily, we have a lot of possible witnesses."

"We do?" I asked her excitedly. "Who?"

Elizabeth smiled and pointed to the giant fish tanks on the wall. "Right there," she said. "Those fish all have eyes. They must have seen something."

I knew what that meant. She wanted me to

interrogate some fish. *Interrogate* is one of the detective words Elizabeth taught me. It means to ask a witness some questions.

I looked around. There didn't seem to be anyone in the hall. This was the perfect time to talk to some fish. I walked over to the saltwater Indian Ocean tank and stuck my face up to the glass so I didn't have to talk too loudly. I didn't want anyone to hear me asking a fish questions. Then I tapped on the glass to get the attention of one or two passing fish.

"Get outta here!" one of the fish shouted at me.

I looked toward the bottom of the tank. There was a fat fish with an angry frown on his face.

"I just want to ask you a question," I told the grumpy fish.

"Would you like it if I came to your house and stuck my face in your window?" he demanded.

I probably wouldn't like that one bit.

"You two-legged air breathers are always banging on our windows and making weird faces at us," the fish continued. "It's annoying!"

"I'm sorry," I said. "I won't bang again, I promise."

"Okay," the grumpy fish said. He began to swim away.

"No! Don't go!" I pleaded. "I need to know something. Did you see anyone steal that big shark tooth?"

The fish rolled his eyes. At least I thought he did. It's hard to tell with a fish. "You air breathers are obsessed with sharks," he said. "Grouper fish are interesting, too."

"I'm sure you are," I said. "But I need to know about that shark tooth."

"Okay," the grouper said. "I didn't see anyone take anything."

"Did any of you see someone steal the tooth?" I asked some other fish swimming by.

"Not me," a flathead fish said.

"Me neither," a moray eel said. "But there was one air breather here after all the other little air breathers left."

"Oh yeah," the grouper said. "The one with the spots and the red scales near the eyes."

Huh? A person with spots and scales? Talk about fishy clues. I'd never seen anyone like that.

Or had I?

Chapter 6

"What do you mean, you think *I* stole the shark tooth?" Elizabeth demanded a few seconds later.

"I didn't say it," I told her. "That grouper fish did. He specifically said red scales. Usually scales are those plate things fish and reptiles have all over them. I know people don't have scales. But they do have hair. So the grouper could have meant red hair — which *you* have."

Elizabeth touched one of her wormy red curls. "That's true," she said. "But —"

"He also said spots," I said, interrupting her. "Spots could mean freckles, which you also definitely have."

"But I couldn't have done it, Jack," Elizabeth told me. "Why not?"

"Well, for one thing, I'm a detective, not a crook,"

Elizabeth said. "And for another, I haven't left your side for one second. You would have seen me."

I frowned. She was right on both counts — as usual. I should have known. Elizabeth is never wrong.

"It wasn't me," Elizabeth insisted.

I nodded. I knew that now. But that meant we were back to having absolutely no suspects. Unless . . .

There was someone else with red hair and freckles at the party. "Maybe he meant Alfred," I told her.

Elizabeth looked so mad, I thought she was going to growl at me. "My little brother?" Her eyes bulged. "You're accusing sweet little Alfred of stealing?"

"I . . . um . . . I'm not accusing him of anything," I said. "But I think we have to talk to him. You know, find out if he saw anything, since he was still down here when the rest of the kids were in the elevator."

"Well, I guess when you put it that way . . ." she said slowly.

"Let's go to the turtle pond," I said.

A few minutes later, Elizabeth, Alfred, and I were standing to the side of the turtle pond, away from all the other kids. I didn't want to embarrass him. I just wanted him to give back the shark tooth — if he was the one who had it.

Alfred had to be the thief. Who else in the aquarium would have red scales by his eyes?

"Alfred, we have to ask you something," Elizabeth said. She sounded a lot nicer than she usually did when we were interrogating suspects. But Alfred was her brother, so I guess that was understandable. "Now, I know you didn't, but, well, we just have to ask if —"

"Did you steal the shark tooth?" I interrupted.

Alfred looked at me. "Why would I do that?" he asked me.

"I don't know," I admitted. "But someone said they saw you in the room where the tooth was before it disappeared. No one else was there but you."

"If no one else was there, how did anyone see me?" Alfred asked.

Man, the kid was smart. But I wasn't about to tell him about my special power.

"That doesn't matter," I said. "The question is, did you take the tooth?"

"I was only alone in that room because everyone else took the elevator," Alfred said. "But I would never touch a tooth. They scare me."

"Shark teeth scare you?" I asked. I wasn't surprised. Shark teeth were pretty sharp.

"*All* teeth scare me," Alfred said.

Now *that* surprised me. "What's so scary about teeth?"

"I don't know," Alfred said. "But I don't like them. Especially when they're loose or have fallen out. I can't even look at teeth that don't have a mouth around them."

"That's true," Elizabeth agreed. "When Alfred lost his first tooth, he put it under my *mother's* pillow for the tooth fairy to find. He had nightmares trying to sleep with it in his bed."

"I'm scared of sharks, too," Alfred said. "I don't even like getting bitten by mosquitoes."

"Mosquitoes don't bite, they sting," I corrected him.

"Well, I don't like them," Alfred said. "And since I'm really scared of sharks and teeth —"

"— there's no way you would steal a shark tooth," I finished his sentence for him.

"Can I go back and look at the turtles?" Alfred asked Elizabeth. "I like when they stick their heads into their shells. I think they're hiding because we scare them."

"Sure, go ahead," Elizabeth told him. As he raced off, she turned and gave me one of her know-it-all smiles. "See? I told you he didn't do it."

"Why didn't you tell me all that stuff about him being scared of teeth before?" I asked her.

"Because you would have thought I was covering for my brother," Elizabeth told me.

She was right. That's exactly what I would have thought. Still, she didn't have to seem so happy. We still had a missing tooth and no suspects.

Just then, Frank the guard walked past us. He pointed to his eyes. Then he pointed to me.

Oh brother. I knew what that meant. There actually *was* a suspect in this crime. And that suspect was me.

"Elizabeth, we've gotta solve this case," I told her. "And fast."

Chapter 7

"We have to get some clues," Elizabeth said with a frown.

"Tell me something I don't know," I replied.

"You could interview more fish," she suggested.

"Fish aren't exactly great at conversation," I told her. "They hate when people bug them through the glass."

"Okay," Elizabeth said. "There are other sea creatures at the aquarium."

"But there's nothing but fish in the room where the shark tooth was," I said. "And if *they* didn't see anyone stealing the tooth —"

"Maybe some other animal noticed something suspicious," Elizabeth interrupted me. "Like someone carrying the tooth, or sneaking around somewhere they shouldn't be. The criminals in mystery books always have some weird behavior that tips off the detectives. You want to talk to some turtles?"

I shook my head. "There are too many people around here. Besides, you heard what Alfred said. They just tuck in their heads when they see something scary. A thief is plenty scary. If one went by, all they would have seen would have been the insides of their shells."

"You have a point," Elizabeth agreed. "Let's wander around. We'll find other animals to talk to."

Unfortunately, everywhere we looked there were aquarium workers. There were members of the cleanup crew by the starfish, and two scientists staring at the moon jellyfish.

"I'm going to be a suspect forever," I groaned.

"Be patient," Elizabeth said. "We'll find a quiet place for you to start interrogating the animals."

We turned and headed down an empty hallway. A blast of freezing cold air hit us hard.

"Hi, you guys," Teddy said, as he walked out into the hallway from a room that must have felt like a refrigerator. "What are you up to?"

"Still trying to figure out who stole that tooth," I said.

"So did you find out?" Teddy asked us.

"Not yet," Elizabeth said. "But we're working on it."

"You should just forget about it," Teddy said

"We can't," I told him. "We're already on the case."

"You didn't see anyone unusual around here today, did you?" Elizabeth asked Teddy.

Teddy shrugged. "Nope. Just aquarium workers — and *you guys*."

I frowned. That made it sound like Teddy suspected me, too.

"What's in there?" Elizabeth asked, pointing toward the cold room.

"Emperor penguins," Teddy said. "I brought them some fish. The more chores I do, the more money I earn toward my bike."

"I guess fish is what penguins eat in Antarctica," Elizabeth said.

"Yep," Teddy said. "The aquarium tries to make their environment as much like their real home as possible. That's why it's so cold in there. I'm going

42

to feed the sea lions next," Teddy said. "You want to help me?"

Elizabeth shook her head. "We have to interrogate possible witnesses," she said. "But we'll definitely see you in the shark tank."

Teddy shrugged and ran his hand over his Mohawk. "Whatever," he said.

As Teddy walked off, Elizabeth grabbed me by the hand. "Come on. Teddy left the door to the penguin environment open. You have to go talk to them."

"No way," I replied. "That room is as cold as Antarctica."

"You have to, Jack," Elizabeth said. "We have to talk to everyone who may have seen or heard something. You never know — maybe the crook hid in the penguin room after the theft."

She was right, and I knew it. So into the cold we went.

"How do those birds stand this?" I grumbled. "It's freezing."

"They have dense feathers that work like a blanket," Elizabeth explained "And sometimes they huddle together to keep warm." She gave me a goofy smile and

twirled her wormy red curls around her finger. "*We* could huddle," she suggested. Then she took the candy cane–striped felt hat out of her backpack and put it on her head. Once again the Brainiac was prepared for anything!

But I didn't have a hat. And I wasn't huddling with her. No way. So the sooner I got out of there, the better. I hurried over to a group of penguins munching on fish.

A penguin looked up from his meal. "Excuse me," he said in a snobby English accent. "Do you have a reservation for dinner?"

I looked at him. "What?"

"This is a very exclusive dinner party," the penguin explained. "Don't you see we are all dressed in tuxedos?"

Their feathers did look like tuxedos. No wonder he sounded so snobby.

"Actually, I'm a detective," I explained. "I need to ask you a few questions."

"I can't believe you're talking to him, Stanley," another snobby penguin said. "He's N-O-K."

"N-O-K?" I asked.

"Not our kind," the penguin said.

45

"Oh. You mean not a penguin," I said. "It's okay. I can understand everything you're saying."

"He meant you're not classy like us," Stanley explained. "That pink T-shirt isn't formal."

Darn T-shirt! It was causing me nothing but trouble.

"I just want to know if anything unusual happened around here today." I tried faking an English accent. It wasn't great, but Stanley *did* answer me.

"Well, our meal server was late, which is unacceptable," Stanley said. "And the girl who usually observes us in the evenings was here in the morning instead."

"Someone observes you?" I asked.

"A girl with no manners," Stanley said. "She stares, which is very rude!"

"What does this starer look like?" I asked.

"She has long, dark feathers on her head, and she's too thin to be in the cold," Stanley said. "She's a penguin wannabe. But who *wouldn't* want to be like us?"

"MOMMMMMMMYYYYYY!"

Suddenly, I heard a loud shout from the other side of the glass.

This interview was over.

Chapter 8

"I wanna play with the penguins! It's *my* birthday! I should be the one who gets to play with the penguins, not Jack and Elizabeth!" Mia whined.

"No one is playing with any penguins," my mother told Mia.

I didn't look at my parents, Mia, or Alyssa. I knew they were all plenty mad. The temperature was a lot warmer in the outer room. But everyone was being really cold to us.

"What were you two doing in there, anyway?" my dad demanded.

"We . . . um . . ." I had no idea what to tell him.

Luckily, Elizabeth was really good at thinking on the spot. "The door to the penguin exhibit was open," she explained. She batted her eyelashes. "We figured we were allowed to go in there just like we could go in any room in the aquarium."

"But that door shouldn't have been open," Alyssa insisted. "It's always locked. We can't just let people wander in there."

"Why not?" Mia asked. "I want to play with the pretty penguins."

Alyssa shook her head. "Emperor penguins don't always like visitors," she told my sister. "And some of those penguins are guarding eggs. They could really cause trouble if they feel those are in danger. That's

PENGUIN
EXHIBIT
KEEP OUT

SHUT

why only people who know how to act around penguins are allowed in there."

I shrugged. "Well, the door was open," I insisted. "So it's not our fault."

"Not *this* time," Frank the guard said. "But you're not fooling me, kid. I'm definitely watching you."

No kidding, I thought to myself. But I didn't say that. I was too afraid to say anything.

A few minutes later, the kindergartners had gone off with Alyssa and my parents to the arts-and-crafts room, and Frank had been called up to check on something on the third floor. That left my partner and me alone.

"Okay, so what did the penguins tell you?" Elizabeth asked me as she opened her notebook.

"I only talked to one," I said. "He said their dinner had been served late, and some woman who usually stares at them at night had been there earlier."

Elizabeth wrote all that down. Then she stared at the clues. "Did he describe the server or the starer?" she asked.

"He said the person who observes them was really thin, and that she had long, dark feathers on her head.

That probably was hair," I added. By now I was used to the way animals described people.

Elizabeth thought about that. "The aquarium is closed to visitors at night," she said. "So whoever this skinny person with long, dark hair is, she must work here."

"There are a lot of people working here," I said.

"But not people who are skinny and have long, dark hair," Elizabeth said. "So far, Alyssa is the only person I've seen who fits that description. The penguin said whoever was staring at them had changed her regular schedule and come to see them earlier in the day instead of at night. The penguin environment is on the same floor as that shark tooth. Maybe she was down here early figuring out how to steal the shark tooth!"

"Alyssa knew a lot about penguins," I told Elizabeth. "Like she knew there were eggs in the environment. I didn't spot any eggs. They must have been hidden. A person would have to be observing the penguins up close for a long time to know about those."

"Exactly," Elizabeth said. "Now you're thinking like a detective!"

That was a big compliment coming from Elizabeth. It really did seem like we had a good suspect this time. *Except . . .*

"Why would Alyssa steal the tooth when everyone was around if she could take it at night when no one was looking?" I asked Elizabeth.

Elizabeth didn't say anything at first. Wow! Was it possible I had just outsmarted the Brainiac?

Nope.

"She was probably trying not to be a suspect," Elizabeth said. "If she stole the shark tooth at night, she'd practically be giving herself away because she's one of the few people here at night. This way she can make it look like there are other people who could be suspects."

"Like me," I said sadly.

"Exactly," Elizabeth agreed. "A schedule change is usually something a criminal does right before she commits a crime. And that's just what Alyssa did. She may be smart enough to work at an aquarium, but I think we may have just outsmarted her!"

Chapter 9

"We can't just ask Alyssa if she stole the tooth. We're going to have to trick her into telling us," Elizabeth explained a few minutes later.

I didn't know how two third graders were going to trick a really smart grown-up into telling us anything, but Elizabeth seemed pretty sure of herself. So I followed her into the arts-and-crafts room, where Mia and her friends were making clay fish.

"Hi, Alyssa," Elizabeth said. "Can I ask you some questions? I'm thinking of being a marine biologist when I grow up."

I gave Elizabeth a funny look. I didn't know that about her.

Elizabeth shot me a sneaky sideways glance.

Oh. She was faking. This was part of her scheme to trick Alyssa into admitting to being the tooth thief.

"Then I'm the right person to ask," Alyssa said. "I'm studying to get my degree in marine biology at the university."

"Awesome," Elizabeth said. "I'm particularly interested in the life cycle of the penguin —"

Just then, Mia got out of her chair and walked over to a fishbowl. "Jack, what are these?" she asked me.

I knew I should be listening to what Alyssa and Elizabeth were saying, but I figured keeping Mia busy was important, too. "They're sea monkeys," I told her. I had once gotten a package of sea monkeys from an ad in a comic book. I knew what they looked like.

"Did he just call us sea monkeys?" I heard one of the sea monkeys say. "We're not monkeys."

"We're brine shrimp," another added. "And proud of it. You don't see us clowning around for bananas, do you?"

"They're also called *brine shrimp*," I told Mia.

"How do you know?" she asked me.

"Um . . . I just do," I told her. "Now, go sit down."

For once Mia did what she was told. "I'm making a monkey," she said as she skipped back to her seat.

Good. Now I could focus on what Elizabeth was asking our suspect.

"Do you get any special privileges because you work here?" Elizabeth wondered.

"You mean like a discount in the gift shop?" Alyssa asked.

"No. More like a chance to hang around the aquarium when no one is around," Elizabeth said.

"Sure," Alyssa said. "Sometimes I stay late to do penguin research."

Wow! I was practically jumping out of my shoes with excitement. Alyssa had admitted to being around the aquarium when no one else was there. We didn't even have to pry it out of her.

"Do you only do research at night?" Elizabeth asked her.

"Usually," Alyssa answered. "But today I came to work before the aquarium even opened to observe the penguins. I had Mia's party and a few other things I wanted to get done ahead of time."

I'll bet, I thought. Things like figure out how to steal a shark tooth and make it look like some innocent kid did it.

"Um . . . do you know how this penguin environment is different from how they live in the wild?" Elizabeth asked her. "Like, does it snow?"

Alyssa shook her head. "It doesn't snow in Antarctica," she explained. "It's actually the driest continent. But . . ."

Just then, a guy in a blue *Friend of the Fishes* shirt walked over to where we were standing. "Alyssa, you can take your fifteen-minute break now," he said. "I'll stay here with the kids."

"Great!" Alyssa exclaimed. She smiled at Elizabeth.

"I have some great pictures of marine life in my locker. Do you want to see them?"

"Sure!" Elizabeth exclaimed.

As we walked out of the room, Elizabeth gave me a knowing smile. I smiled back. A locker would be the perfect place for a crook to stash a stolen tooth.

Amazing! Elizabeth had tricked Alyssa into giving herself away. In a few minutes we would have the tooth in hand.

This was just too easy.

"Here we go!" Alyssa exclaimed a minute later as she opened her locker.

Elizabeth and I nearly bashed into each other trying to look inside. Unfortunately, all we saw were books and photos. No shark tooth.

"Wild emperor penguins," Alyssa said, pointing to a photo. "Someday I'd like to visit them in Antarctica."

Just then Alyssa's phone buzzed. She looked at the text message. "The kids are ready for their puppet show. I have to go. This has been fun. It's the first break I've had since the kids arrived."

I tried to stop her, but Elizabeth shook her head. "It's okay," she whispered.

As Alyssa walked off, I glared at Elizabeth. "What do you mean, 'it's okay'? We didn't find the tooth."

"Alyssa can't be the thief," Elizabeth told me. "Didn't you hear her? She's been with the party kids all morning without any breaks," Elizabeth explained. "The tooth disappeared *after* the party started. She didn't have time to steal it."

"So we're back to square one?" I asked.

Elizabeth nodded sadly. "But maybe the sharks will have some clues."

Talk to the sharks, huh? Well, that sounded like a good idea.

Except for one very *big* problem.

Chapter 10

"How am I supposed to talk to the sharks?" I asked Elizabeth. "If I try to open my mouth underwater, I'll drown."

"I never thought of that," Elizabeth admitted.

Of course she hadn't. *She* didn't have to. But those are the kinds of things a guy has to think about when he can talk to animals.

"How about you interview a shark *before* you get in? You can stand by the side of the giant pool and talk to the sharks that swim by," Elizabeth suggested.

"But I want to swim with the sharks," I said. "I should get to do something fun today."

"Solving a mystery is fun," Elizabeth said.

I shook my head. "Mysteries are a lot more fun to

solve when you're not the one being accused of the crime," I told her.

"I know," Elizabeth agreed. "Look, just find some shark, talk to him quickly, and then you can get in and swim."

"I guess that works," I said.

Teddy was already in his black diving suit when Elizabeth and I reached the pool area a few minutes later. "What took you two so long?" Teddy asked us.

"We were interrogating a suspect," Elizabeth told him.

"The *wrong* suspect," I added. "This is one tough case."

Teddy put his face mask over his eyes and grabbed a snorkel. "Forget about the case," he said. "Let's go swim with some sharks." And with that, he got into the water and began swimming around.

"He looks like a professional," I said.

"That's because he gets to do this all the time," Elizabeth pointed out. "I'm going to swim with him for a few minutes, just so he's distracted. Then you'll be free to talk to a shark."

It sounded like a plan. A plan that meant I did all the work while Elizabeth had all the fun. But what could I do? It's not like she could talk to the sharks.

As Elizabeth got in to swim, I went over and sat on the edge of the large tank. I let my feet dangle in the water, and then waited for a shark to notice me.

"Are you getting in?" a lifeguard asked me.

"In a minute," I told him. "I'm . . . um . . . I'm just getting used to the water."

"Okay," the lifeguard said. "Take your time."

I hope it didn't take a lot of time. Elizabeth and Teddy sure seemed to be having a blast. I really wanted to get in and swim with them.

Just then, a baby shark swam by.

"Excuse me," I called out to him, trying not to be so loud that the lifeguard could hear. "I need to ask you something."

The little shark stopped swimming. He cocked his head and looked at me curiously. "Did you just talk to me?" he asked.

I nodded. "Yep."

"Wow. None of the frog people have ever done that before," he said.

Frog people? I looked down at the big black fins I was wearing on my feet. They were kind of froglike, actually.

"You're not here to steal my loose tooth, are you?" the shark asked me. "Because I'm not giving it up without a fight."

He didn't have to worry. I wasn't about to fight a shark.

"You have a loose tooth?" I asked him.

He nodded, and the big dorsal fin on his back went up and down. Then he opened his mouth wide so I could see. I jumped back a little. There were a whole lot of sharp teeth in there.

"It's my first loose tooth," the little shark told me. "As soon as it falls out, I'm going to hide it under a rock so the sea tooth fairy can find it."

"The sea tooth fairy?" I asked him.

"She collects shark teeth that have fallen out and leaves yummy fish in their place," he explained. "Only I won't get the fish if the mean frog man steals my tooth instead."

"What mean frog man?" I asked.

"The one who was here before, taking teeth from

the bottom of the tank," the baby shark told me. "He steals them."

The little shark was right. That frog man did sound really mean. Mean enough to have stolen the shark tooth fossil, and leave me to take the blame.

I'd obviously gotten all I could out of that shark. So as he swam off, I put on my goggles and dove into the tank. It was time for me to swim with the sharks.

Splash! The minute I hit the water, two sharks swam right for me. I waved.

"There goes another frog man clowning around," one of them said as he swam past me.

"You know why the shark spit out the clown?" his friend asked him. "Because he tasted funny!"

The two sharks laughed as they swam off. I laughed, too — and got a big mouthful of salt water. *Blech!*

Just then, Elizabeth swam over to me. She used her finger to draw a question mark in the water. I knew she was asking me if I had gotten any information from the questions I'd asked the shark.

I nodded. I definitely had some clues. And they were just the kind a girl like Elizabeth could really sink her teeth into!

Chapter 11

"It sure took you long enough to get into the water," Teddy said later as he hung up his snorkel gear in the changing room.

"Yeah," I admitted. "But it was worth it." I was talking about the fact that I'd gotten a good clue from that baby shark. But Teddy didn't know that. He thought I was talking about swimming, which was also pretty cool. I'd never been that close to so many fish in my whole life.

"I know," Teddy said. "Those sharks are incredible. You ever see so many teeth in one mouth before?"

I shook my head. "Weird how they have so many rows of them."

Teddy nodded. "Yup. One falls out and another just slides into place." He put some hair gel on his head and made his Mohawk stand up. "Well, it was good swimming with you. I'll probably see you around before your sister's party is over."

"Yeah," I said. "See you later."

I left the boys' changing room a few minutes after Teddy. Elizabeth was already in the hall waiting for me. Her red, wormy curls were still sopping wet.

"So?" she asked me excitedly. "What did you find out?"

"There's a shark tooth thief around here, that's for sure," I told her.

Elizabeth rolled her eyes. "No kidding," she said.

"No, I mean *new* shark teeth," I explained. "Not the fossil kind. There's a diver who's swiping shark teeth from the bottom of the shark tank."

Elizabeth wrote that down in her notebook. "Someone who is that interested in new shark teeth would probably be quadruple interested in a giant fossilized shark tooth."

I didn't know exactly what *quadruple* interested meant, but I figured it had something to do with being really, really interested. So I nodded. "That's exactly what I thought," I said.

"This is just a start," Elizabeth continued. "There are a whole lot of people diving in and out of that tank. People who work here and visitors. It doesn't really narrow it down as much as I would like."

Elizabeth was right, of course. When wasn't she? My grin faded.

"But we're closer than we were before," Elizabeth assured me. "A few more clues and we'll have this thing wrapped up."

That was easy for her to say. She wasn't the one who was going to have to interview the animals to find those clues. That job was all mine.

"Go talk to them." Elizabeth pushed me toward the outdoor sea lion tank a few minutes later. "I don't know how much longer it will be before their next show. And once that happens, there will be a lot of people around here." She turned around and pointed to the bleachers that surrounded the sea lion tank.

Elizabeth had a point. Once the show started, all those seats would be full. And I didn't want my talking to animals to be part of the show. So I walked over to the big tank and stood on the cement stage near the water.

The sea lions were nearby, tossing a ball around with their noses.

"Hey! Heads up!" one of them called out suddenly.

A huge beach ball sailed right for me. I reached out my arms and caught it.

"Nice catch," a dark brown sea lion said.

"Thanks," I said. "I play a lot of baseball."

"Nah, he did it all wrong," a spotted sea lion argued. "He was supposed to catch it with his nose." He turned

CLAP
CLAP

to the dark brown sea lion. "That's why I don't want any flipperless folks in our act. *Sheesh.* Everyone wants to be in showbiz."

"I don't want to be in showbiz," I said.

A really chubby sea lion smiled at me. "I know, you want an autograph," she purred. "All my fans want an autograph. Not that I blame you. I'm the star of this show."

"You are not," the spotted sea lion told her. "Just because you do that one flip at the end doesn't make you the star." He looked at me. "I'm the one whose autograph you want, kid."

The spotted sea lion tossed the ball to the chubby sea lion. She twirled around and caught it on her nose. Then she smiled and gave a little bow.

I just stood there.

"Don't I get some applause?" the chubby sea lion asked me. "My adoring fans always applaud for me."

"Maybe he's not so adoring," the dark brown sea lion told her.

"Then he's not getting my autograph," the chubby sea lion said.

Frankly, I wasn't sure how she could give me an autograph, anyway. It wasn't like sea lions had fingers to write with.

Besides, autographs were the last things on my mind. What I needed right now were answers.

Chapter 12

"What are those sea lions saying?" Elizabeth asked me. She was sitting in the bleachers near the tank with her notebook and pen in her hands.

"I don't know if they're going to be any help," I called back nervously to her.

"What do you mean we won't be any help?" the chubby sea lion demanded. "Celebrities are very helpful."

I didn't think the sea lion was exactly a celebrity, but I knew if I was going to get any answers, I was going to have to play along.

"Oh, I know," I told her. "Celebrities help kids all over the world."

"And you're a kid," the chubby sea lion said. "So how can I help?"

"Well, I was wondering — have you seen anyone around here carrying a giant ancient tooth?" I asked.

All three sea lions stopped and stared at me.

"What, is this some sort of joke?" the dark brown sea lion asked.

"I bet we're on a TV show," the spotted sea lion said. "You're playing a prank, right?"

"Where are the cameras?" the chubby sea lion asked excitedly.

"It's not a TV show," I said. "I really need to know. Have you seen anyone carrying a tooth? Or just something weird going on lately?"

"Well, there was that one thing," the dark brown sea lion said.

"It was no big deal," the spotted sea lion added.

"I hardly even noticed," the chubby sea lion said.

"What? What?" I asked the sea lions impatiently.

"Well, it's just that there's this shack back there behind the bushes," the spotted sea lion said. "No one has been there for years. Most folks have forgotten it even exists. But someone has been going back there every afternoon for the past week."

"Oh, that's good," I said. I turned to Elizabeth. "Write that down."

"Write *what* down?" she asked me. "All I heard was a bunch of squeaking and barking. Sea lion noises."

Oh yeah. I forgot Elizabeth couldn't understand what the sea lions were saying.

"There's a shack back there that's been abandoned for years, but someone has been going in and out of there all week long," I told Elizabeth. "A shack would be a great place to stash stolen stuff."

"Definitely," Elizabeth agreed. "Ask them what the person looked like."

Oh right. That would help. "What did the person going into the shack look like?" I asked the sea lions.

"Well, he was a flipperless fellow, like you," the spotted sea lion said. "But there was something strange about him."

"Oh yes, it was strange," the chocolate sea lion agreed.

"Very strange," the chubby sea lion added.

"WHAT WAS STRANGE?" I shouted. I was getting very frustrated.

"He had a dorsal fin," the spotted sea lion said. "Right on the top of his head. I've never seen a flipperless fellow with a dorsal fin before."

Neither had I. In fact, the whole thing sounded fishy to me. But I didn't want to insult the sea lions again. So I just nodded and said, "Thanks for your help." Although I didn't really think they'd been much help at all.

"I don't know why we're even bothering investigating that shack," I said to Elizabeth a few minutes later. "Those sea lions were nuts. A human with a dorsal fin on his head? That's not possible."

"It might be," Elizabeth said.

"In some weird horror movie, maybe," I told her. "But in real life, I don't think so."

"You have to think like a sea lion," Elizabeth reminded me. "To a sea lion, hair could *look* like a dorsal fin, if it was sticking straight up."

"Like a Mohawk!" I exclaimed excitedly. Suddenly I understood what Elizabeth was thinking. "Do you think Teddy could be the thief?"

"It's possible," Elizabeth said. "He does know a lot about shark teeth. And he's mentioned going to see a sea lion show or feeding the sea lions. So he's around here often. He had plenty of time to find the shack."

"And he swims in the shark tank a lot," I added. "So he could be the one stealing all the teeth from under rocks."

"Exactly," Elizabeth agreed. "Now we just have to prove it."

Chapter 13

"Okay, this place is creepy," I said as Elizabeth and I walked into the old shack. "Let's get out of here."

"Not until we find that giant tooth," Elizabeth said. She lifted a blanket off the floor. About a hundred cockroaches came racing out.

"Hey! Who turned on the lights?" I heard one of them yell.

"Scatter before they start that *Cucaracha* dance!" another shouted. "I don't want to get stepped on."

"No one's stepping on you," I told the cockroach.

"Huh?" Elizabeth asked.

Oops. I'd forgotten Elizabeth couldn't hear the cockroaches. "Never mind," I said.

"Well, well, what have we here?" Elizabeth said, walking over to a large brown grocery bag. She sounded just like a detective on TV. "Just as I thought. Shark teeth!"

I peered into the bag. There were at least 40 shark teeth inside. "This is Alfred's worst nightmare," I joked. "A bag full of teeth."

Elizabeth frowned. "Don't make fun of my little brother," she said.

Sheesh. She sure could be sensitive. But I didn't want to argue with the only person in the whole aquarium who knew I was innocent of stealing the giant shark tooth fossil. So I apologized.

"Sorry," I said. Then I opened a closet door and peeked inside.

And there, on the floor, hidden in a corner of the closet, was the fossilized shark tooth!

"Jackpot!" I shouted. "I found it!"

Elizabeth rushed over. "Yep, that's it," she said as I pulled the giant tooth out into the light.

"Come on," I said. "Let's get out of here and give this to that guard. I can't wait to clear my name."

"That won't clear your name," Elizabeth told me.

Huh?

"Everyone will just think you took it, and now you're

giving it back," Elizabeth told me. "We have to prove that Teddy was the crook."

Oh man. I hate when the Brainiac is right.

"So how are we going to prove that?" I asked.

"Teddy is going to come back here for the tooth, and we'll be here waiting for him," Elizabeth told me. "Let's hide in the closet. That way we can pop out when he arrives and surprise him. The element of surprise is important when you're trying to catch a criminal. Detectives in books surprise crooks all the time."

She sounded really sure Teddy would show up at the shack. That made me nervous. "What are we supposed to do when he gets here?" I asked her. "He's older than we are. And bigger. He could go crazy on us."

Elizabeth didn't say anything. I guess she hadn't thought about that possibility. People don't usually go crazy on kids in books that are written *for* kids. But this was no book. This was real life. And that meant anything was possible.

But I went into the closet and hid next to Elizabeth just the same. I couldn't just leave my partner to face a crazy tooth-stealing crook alone.

Elizabeth gave me one of her weird smiles and twirled one of her wormy curls around her finger.

Ugh. I hated when Elizabeth acted like that. I sure hoped Teddy didn't take a long time getting here.

Creak. Just then, the door to the shack opened and somebody came inside. I peeked through a slit in the closet door. Sure enough, it was a flipperless fellow with a dorsal fin on his head — *otherwise known as Teddy*.

Elizabeth sprang into action. She flung the closet door open and leaped out. "Stop right there!" she shouted at Teddy.

I just stood there, frozen, staring out at them from the closet. My feet wouldn't move.

"What are you two doing here?" Teddy asked. He didn't sound mad, or even scared. In fact, he was perfectly calm, which was weird since we'd just caught him sneaking into a shack full of stolen shark teeth.

"We're here to get back the giant shark tooth fossil so we can clear Jack's name," Elizabeth told him. "We already found the fossil. And now we know for sure who the real thief is."

"It's you," I said. "And we're telling."

Teddy stared at us for a minute. His eyes got kind of small, and his lips scrunched up tight. He looked the way my mom did that day she found Leo and I using chocolate sauce to paint my room brown. She had looked really, *really* angry.

My heart started pounding.

Teddy took a step toward us. And another. And then, he looked me right in the eye and . . . he began to laugh.

Chapter 14

"What's so funny?" I demanded.

"You two are," Teddy said. "Playing detective."

"We're not playing," I shouted at him. "We *are* detectives."

"Okay, *detectives*," Teddy demanded. "Tell me what reason I would have for stealing a tooth fossil."

"Well ... um ... you ..." He had me there. I had no idea what his motive might be.

Luckily, Elizabeth had figured that part out. She turned back a few pages in her notebook and smiled. "You told us your motive when we met you," she said. "You want to buy a bicycle. And it would take way too long to earn enough money doing chores around here. But selling a fossilized shark tooth and some shark tooth necklaces would get you the money fast."

Teddy gave her a slow, evil smile. "Impressive thinking," he said. "But you're wrong. I have no interest in shark teeth."

"Really?" Elizabeth asked him. "Then what's that in your jacket pocket?"

I looked at Teddy. I hadn't noticed it before, but one of his pockets was bulging.

"None of your business," Teddy said.

"I think it is," Elizabeth said. Before Teddy could stop her, Elizabeth reached in and pulled out a clear plastic bag full of shark tooth necklaces.

"Give that back!" Teddy shouted at her.

"Not a chance," Elizabeth said as she held up a shark tooth that was strung onto a piece of black cord. "We've proved you're the crook now. You're making and selling shark tooth necklaces. But that wasn't enough. You had to steal the fossil to make sure you had enough cash for the bike."

Teddy stepped back, ran his hands over his Mohawk, and gave us another evil grin. "Okay, so you got me. I did it. But that isn't going to do you any good."

"Sure it will," I said. "We're going to turn you in."

"Go ahead," Teddy said. "Everyone will still think

you're the crook. They'll think you're just blaming it on me."

"But we both heard you admit it," I insisted. "It's two against one."

"Yeah, but she's your girlfriend," Teddy said.

"She is NOT my girlfriend!" I shouted. "She's my detective partner." Why couldn't anybody get that straight?

"Whatever," Teddy answered. "It doesn't matter what you call her. Everyone will still think she's your accomplice."

"My what?" I asked. I hadn't heard that word before.

"Accomplice," Elizabeth repeated. "Someone who helps a criminal commit a crime." She looked kind of sad. Probably because she knew Teddy was right.

"It's my word against yours," Teddy told me. "And who do you think the people here are going to believe? Someone who has grown up around the aquarium, or some stranger who everyone already thinks is a thief?"

Oh man. No one was ever going to believe us. Ever. This really stunk.

Teddy just stood there, smiling. "Now I'm getting out of here," he said. He gave us one last grin as he headed for the door. He knew he had us.

At least, he thought he did. Then, suddenly, someone else stepped into the shack.

"Not so fast, Teddy," she said. "These two kids aren't the only witnesses here. I heard every word you said."

Chapter 15

"Alyssa!" I shouted. Boy, was I glad to see her.

Elizabeth gave me a big smile. We both knew that the aquarium would believe Alyssa over Teddy any day. She was an adult. And she hadn't been caught red-handed, the way he had.

"What are you doing here?" Teddy asked her.

"I was looking for Jack and Elizabeth, to tell them it was almost time for Mia's birthday cake," Alyssa said. "I heard some people arguing in the shack, so I walked over to see what the trouble was. And I definitely found a troublemaker."

Teddy just looked at her. He didn't seem very scary anymore. Instead, he looked scared himself.

Alyssa took the giant shark tooth fossil from my hands. "Okay, Teddy. You and I are going to put this

back where it belongs. And then we're going to give all those shark teeth over to the aquarium shop, where they can sell them to raise money to take care of the shark tank and buy more fish treats for the sharks."

I grinned. I knew that little shark would like that a lot. He'd probably think the sea tooth fairy had brought the fish treats just for him.

"And then we're going to go tell your dad what happened," Alyssa told him. "He's not going to be happy."

Teddy didn't say anything. He just followed Alyssa glumly out of the shack. Then he turned and glared at Elizabeth and me.

"Why couldn't you just stay out of it?" he asked us angrily.

"Because we're detectives," I told him. "And solving cases is what we do."

"Well, Jack, I guess we all owe you an apology," Alyssa said a few minutes later. We were standing in the long hallway where the fish tanks were. Mia and her friends had gathered around us. The giant shark tooth was back where it belonged.

Frank the guard looked at me and grumbled. It was probably as close to an apology as he'd ever given.

"To show you how grateful we are that you two found the fossil, I am giving you each a lifetime family pass to the aquarium." Alyssa handed plastic guest passes to Elizabeth and me.

"Does this mean I can come and swim with the sharks again?" I asked.

"And I can study some of the sea life?" Elizabeth wondered.

"Any time you like," Alyssa assured us.

"MOM! I want a guest pass," Mia the Pain whined. "It's my birthday. I should have the guest pass!"

"It's a family pass, Mia," my mother said. "We can all use it."

"But I want to hold it," Mia whined.

I shook my head. Birthday or no birthday, Mia wasn't getting her hands on the pass I'd worked so hard for.

"Let's have some birthday cake," Alyssa suggested. "And we'll all sing to Mia."

A huge grin formed on my sister's face. There was nothing she liked more than being the center of attention.

We all walked over to a table that had been set up near the tanks. Mia's fish-shaped cake was covered with seven candles — six years and one for good luck.

"Come on everyone, let's sing!" Alyssa said. "*Happy birthday to you . . .*"

Mia stood there, smiling and waving her hands up and down like she was conducting an orchestra.

Just then, my attention drifted away from Mia. I heard two familiar voices coming from the fish tank on the wall.

"So, did you hear what Ollie the octopus said when he asked Sally the squid on a date?" Hoho the clown fish asked.

"No. What?" Bobo wondered.

"I want to hold your hand, hand, hand, hand, hand, hand, hand, hand," Hoho answered.

I started laughing. That was a funny one!

"MOM!" Mia stopped blowing out her candles and shouted. "Jack's laughing at me."

I rolled my eyes. Now this was a real mystery: how to stop Mia the Pain from *being* a pain.

But I had a feeling that was one case nobody would ever be able to solve — not even amazing detectives like the Brainiac and me!

CALLING ALL DETECTIVES!

Be sure to read all the
JACK GETS A CLUE mysteries!

The Case of the Beagle Burglar

The Case of the Tortoise in Trouble

The Case of the Green Guinea Pig

The Case of the Loose-Toothed Shark